The Three Little Pigs

Retold by Vera Southgate M.A., B.COM
with illustrations by Sarah Preston

LADYBIRD ✿ TALES

ONCE UPON A TIME there was a mother pig who had three little pigs.

The three little pigs grew so big that their mother said to them, "You are too big to live here any longer. You must go and build houses for yourselves. But take care that the wolf does not catch you."

The three little pigs set off. "We will take care that the wolf does not catch us," they said.

Soon they met a man who was carrying some straw. "Please will you give me some straw?" asked the first little pig. "I want to build a house for myself."

"Yes," said the man and he gave the first little pig some straw.

Then the first little pig built
himself a house of straw. He was
very pleased with his house.
He said, "Now the wolf won't
catch me and eat me."

"I shall build a stronger house than
yours," said the second little pig.

"I shall build a stronger house than
yours, too," said the third little pig.

The second little pig and the third little pig went on along the road. Soon they met a man who was carrying some sticks.

"Please will you give me some sticks?" asked the second little pig. "I want to build a house for myself."

"Yes," said the man and he gave the second little pig some sticks.

Then the second little pig built himself a house of sticks. It was stronger than the house of straw.

The second little pig was very pleased with his house. He said, "Now the wolf won't catch me and eat me."

"I shall build a stronger house than yours," said the third little pig.

The third little pig walked on along the road by himself. Soon he met a man who was carrying some bricks.

"Please will you give me some bricks?" asked the third little pig. "I want to build a house for myself."

"Yes," said the man and he gave the third little pig some bricks.

Then the third little pig built himself a house of bricks.

It took him a long time to build it, for it was a very strong house.

The third little pig was very pleased with his house. He said, "Now the wolf won't catch me and eat me."

The next day the wolf came along the road. He came to the house of straw which the first little pig had built.

When the first little pig saw the wolf coming, he ran inside his house and shut the door.

The wolf knocked on the door and said, "Little pig, little pig, let me come in."

"No, no," said the first little pig. "By the hair of my chinny chin chin, I will not let you come in."

"Then I'll huff and I'll puff and I'll blow your house in," said the wolf.

So he huffed and he puffed and he huffed and he puffed. The house of straw fell down and the wolf ate up the first little pig.

The next day the wolf walked further along the road. He came to the house of sticks which the second little pig had built.

When the second little pig saw the wolf coming, he ran inside his house and shut the door.

The wolf knocked on the door and said, "Little pig, little pig, let me come in."

"No, no," said the second little pig. "By the hair of my chinny chin chin, I will not let you come in."

"Then I'll huff and I'll puff and I'll blow your house in," said the wolf.

So he huffed and he puffed and he huffed and he puffed. The house of sticks fell down and the wolf ate up the second little pig.

The next day the wolf walked further along the road. He came to the house of bricks which the third little pig had built.

When the third little pig saw the wolf coming, he ran inside his house and shut the door.

The wolf knocked on the door and said, "Little pig, little pig, let me come in."

"No, no," said the third little pig. "By the hair of my chinny chin chin, I will not let you come in."

"Then I'll huff and I'll puff and I'll blow your house in," said the wolf.

So he huffed and he puffed and he huffed and he puffed. But the house of bricks did not fall down.

The wolf was very angry, but he pretended not to be. "Little pig," he said, "be ready at six o'clock in the morning and I will take you to Farmer Smith's field. We shall find some nice turnips for dinner."

"Very well," said the little pig. But he was a clever pig. He knew that the wolf just wanted to eat him.

So the next morning the third little pig set off for Farmer Smith's field at five o'clock. He filled his basket with turnips. Then he hurried home before six o'clock.

At six o'clock the wolf knocked on the little pig's door. "Are you ready, little pig?" he said.

"Oh! I have been to Farmer Smith's field," said the little pig. "I filled my basket with turnips and they are now cooking for my dinner."

The wolf was very angry, but he pretended not to be.

Then the wolf said, "Be ready at five o'clock in the morning and I will take you to Farmer Brown's apple tree. We will pick some red apples."

"Very well," said the third little pig.

Next morning the little pig set off at four o'clock. He found the apple tree. He was up in the tree picking apples when the wolf came along.

The little pig was very frightened, but he pretended not to be. He said, "These are fine apples, Mr Wolf. I'll throw you one."

He threw down an apple, but it rolled away down the road. The wolf ran after it.

Then the little pig jumped down from the tree. He ran all the way home and shut his door quickly.

The wolf was very angry, but he still pretended not to be.

He went to the little pig's house and knocked on the door. "Little pig," he said, "be ready at four o'clock this afternoon and I will take you to the fair. We will have some fun on the swings and roundabouts."

"Very well," said the little pig.

At two o'clock the little pig set off for the fair. He had great fun, riding on the swings and roundabouts.

Then he bought himself a butter churn. It looked like a big barrel.

As the little pig was going home he saw the wolf coming up the hill. The little pig was very frightened, so he jumped inside his butter churn.

The butter churn began to roll over and over down the hill. It rolled faster and faster. It knocked the wolf down.

The wolf was so frightened that he ran away as quickly as he could.

The little pig jumped out of his butter churn and carried it home.

The next day the wolf came and knocked on the little pig's door.

He said, "Little pig, I did not go to the fair yesterday. A great big thing came rolling down the hill and knocked me over."

"Ha-ha!" said the little pig. "That was me, inside my butter churn!"

When the wolf heard this he was very, very, very angry indeed.

He said, "Little pig, I am going to eat you up. I am going to climb down your chimney to get you."

The little pig was very frightened, but he said nothing. He put a big pot of water on the fire to boil.

The wolf climbed onto the roof. Then he began to come down the chimney.

The little pig took the lid from the pot. Into the pot fell the wolf, with a big SPLASH!

That was the end of the wolf, and the third little pig lived happily ever after.

A History of The Three Little Pigs

The earliest printed version of this much-loved tale was written by James Orchard Halliwell (an English Shakespearean scholar), and dates back to the 1840s.

Another version from the 1880s has the wolf as a fox, and names the pigs Browny, Whitey and Blacky. Almost ten years later, the story in its best-known form appeared in *English Fairy Tales* by Joseph Jacobs. This story includes the familiar phrases:

"By the hair of my chinny chin chin."

"Then I'll huff and I'll puff and I'll blow your house in!"

A cartoon of the story was made in 1933, and included the popular song, *Who's Afraid of the Big Bad Wolf?*

The tale was confirmed as a childhood favourite in the 1960s with the publication of Ladybird's Well-Loved Tales edition, retold by Vera Southgate and illustrated by Robert Lumley.

Collect more fantastic
LADYBIRD 🐞 TALES

9781409314134

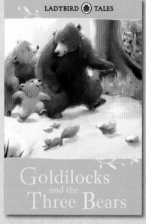

9781409314141

9781409314165

9781409314172